For Shadra, who went on an adventure with me
for this story at the beginning of the process

That's My Carrot!

Story and illustrations by IL SUNG NA

Alfred A. Knopf · New York

I **LOVE** carrots.
I am an expert at growing them.

But something **STRANGE**
is going on in my garden.

I **LOVE** carrots.
I am the best at growing them.

But something **ISN'T RIGHT** in my backyard.

A few days later . . .

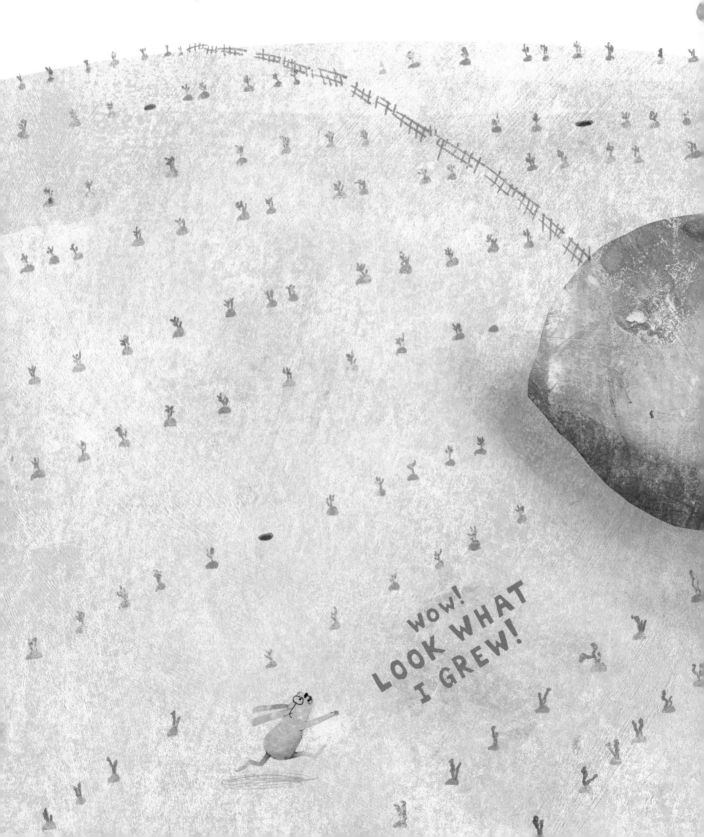

That's MY carrot.

It's on **MY** side!

I'LL DIG

That's MY carrot.

It's on **MY** side!

IT UP!

This is **MY** carrot.

This is **MY** carrot.

I'LL get it!

NO, I can dig it up!

I'VE GOT IT!

THAT'S

MY

where's the carrot?

our carrot

I'm going down there.

is
gone.

I'm going down there, too.

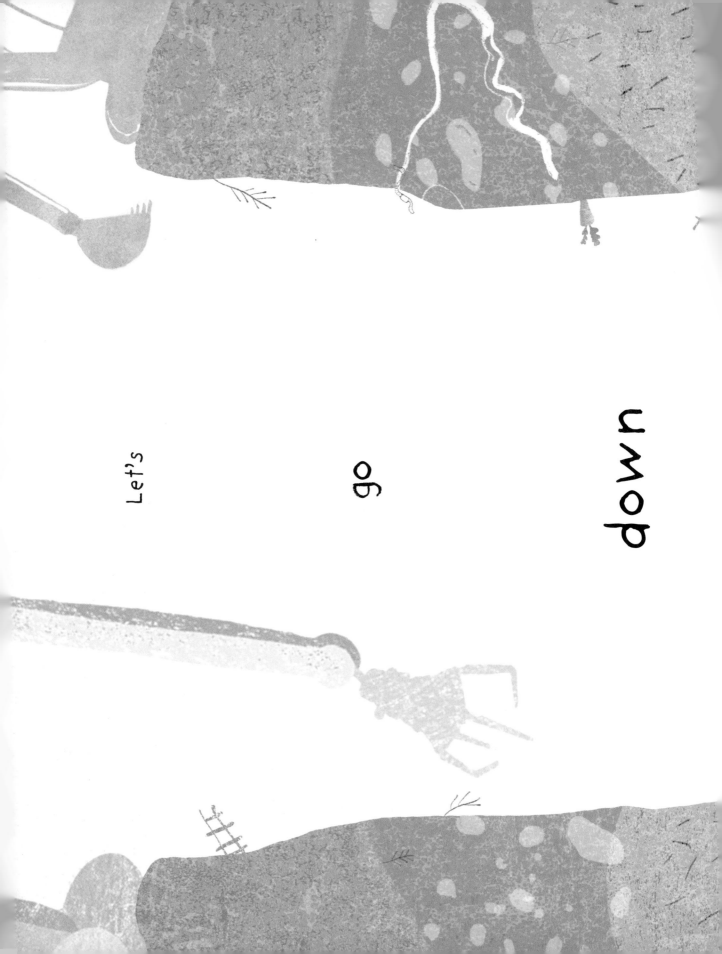

Let's go down

TOGETHER.

Look at these **TUNNELS**!

Under **OUR** fence.

WHERE did they come from?

Are we **THERE** yet?

How **LONG** have we been walking?

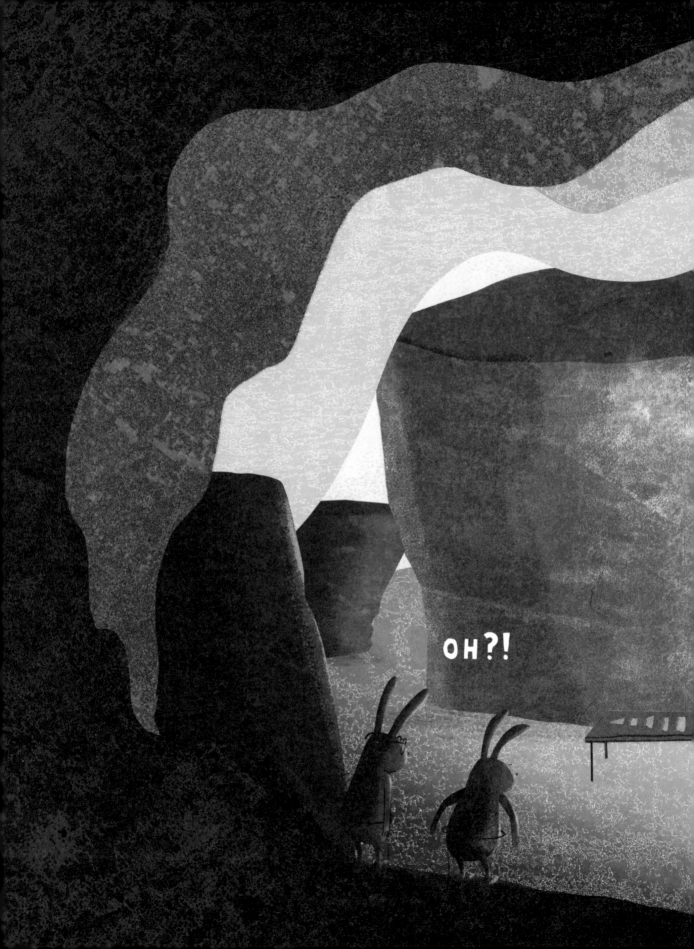

WELCOME!
You're just in time
for carrot soup!

We **LOVE** carrots.

Now we can be experts
at **SHARING** them.

THIS IS A BORZOI BOOK PUBLISHED BY ALFRED A. KNOPF

Copyright © 2020 by Il Sung Na

All rights reserved. Published in the United States by Alfred A. Knopf,
an imprint of Random House Children's Books, a division of
Penguin Random House LLC, New York.

Knopf, Borzoi Books, and the colophon are registered trademarks
of Penguin Random House LLC.

Visit us on the Web! rhcbooks.com
Educators and librarians, for a variety of teaching tools,
visit us at RHTeachersLibrarians.com

Library of Congress Cataloging-in-Publication Data is available upon request.
ISBN 978-0-399-55158-1 (trade) — ISBN 978-0-399-55159-8 (lib. bdg.) —
ISBN 978-0-399-55160-4 (ebook)

MANUFACTURED IN CHINA
May 2020
10 9 8 7 6 5 4 3 2 1
First Edition